W9-CPD-931

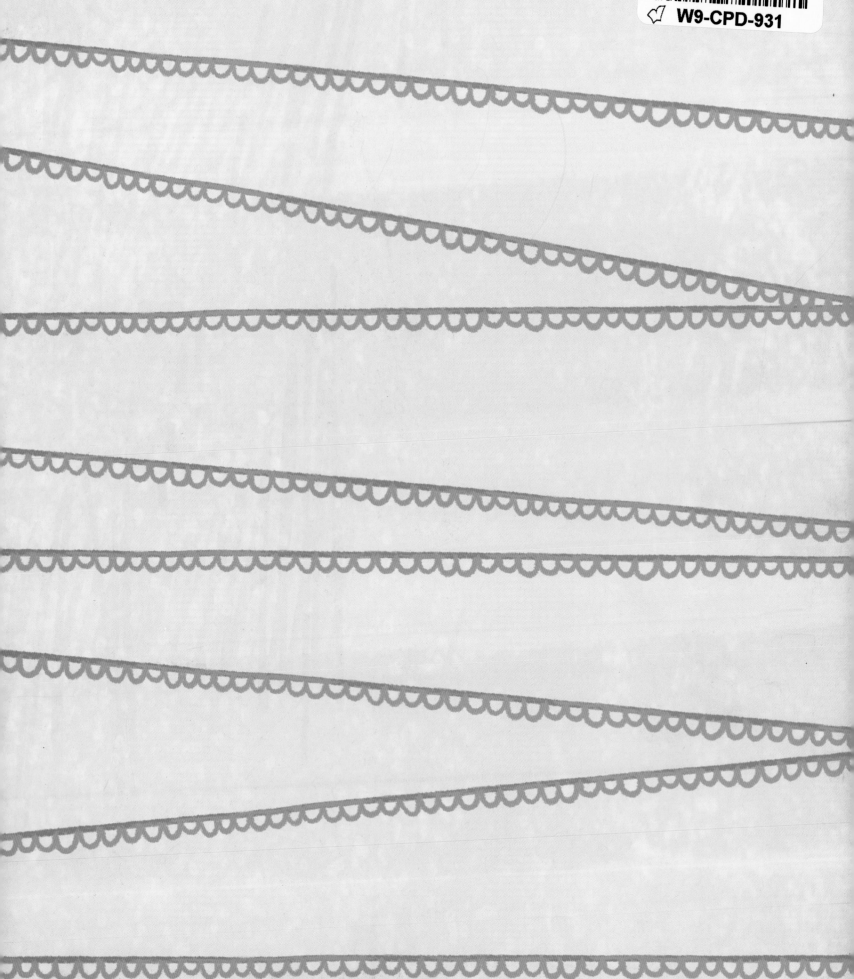

For Avery and Henry, who are both cock-a-doo-delightful! – S.S.

To my smart family and friends who understand that
drawing animals and poop is the best job ever – F.W.

tiger tales
5 River Road, Suite 128, Wilton, CT 06897
Published in the United States 2018
Originally published in Great Britain 2018
by Little Tiger Press
Text copyright © 2018 Steve Smallman
Illustrations copyright © 2018 Florence Weiser
ISBN-13: 978-1-68010-080-8
ISBN-10: 1-68010-080-7
Printed in China
LTP/1400/1977/0917
All rights reserved
10 9 8 7 6 5 4 3 2 1

For more insight and activities,
visit us at www.tigertalesbooks.com

CoCk-a-dOoDle-Poo!

by Steve Smallman

Illustrated by
Florence Weiser

tiger tales

Down on the farm there's a **terrible smell.**
(The cow is pooping and the sheep as well!)

Splat!

"Oh, my!"

It's a large cow pie,

And
the sheep
are popping
out
pellets
that fly!

Pig keeps **plopping** like he's never, ever stopping,
And you'd better stand clear
when a horse's poop is
dropping!

Farmer Jill says,
"What you have to understand
Is that it might **smell** a bit,
but it's **good for the land!**"

But it wasn't so good for
the chickens on the ground,

Stepping over piles
of poo lying
all around!

"Oh, I wish I could fly
where the air is clear,"
groaned Rooster.

"The smell
is just
too strong
down here!"

One day, Farmer Jill came back from the city.
With a new hairstyle, she looked so **pretty!**

Then somebody cried out,

"CoCk-a- dOoDle- dOOoOO!"

And **plopped** on the top
of her nice
new **hairdo!**

She looked at the animals and she said,
"I need to know—who just poOped on my head?"

Horse said, "I heard 'CoCk-a-dOoDle-dooooO!'"

"Rooster!" Sheep cried.
"That's what **YOU** do!"

"Well, it can't be **him!**"
said Hen with a smirk.

"Everybody knows that
his wings don't work.

Chickens can run,
and flap, and JUMP!

But we can't fly high because
we're just too
plump!"

Jill shampooed
the POO from her hair,

And then cried,
"What happened
to my
UNDERWEAR?

I left a pair on the line to dry.
So where did they go?
Underpants can't fly!"

Rooster was hiding;
he felt really bad.
He hadn't meant to poop
on the farmer, but he had.

First he took her **underwear**
and pulled out **the elastic**

To make a **rooster**
booster
catapult.
(It was fantastic!)

It sho'

im up into the sky—

he flew a loOp -the- loOp
and cried out, "CoCk-a-dOoDle-dOo!"

but then he had to poOp!

"From now on," he decided,
"I will only fly at night
In case I have another little
accident in flight!"

He waited 'til the **moon** came out
So he could fly once more—
then saw a fox was sneaking

to the
creaking
henhouse
door!

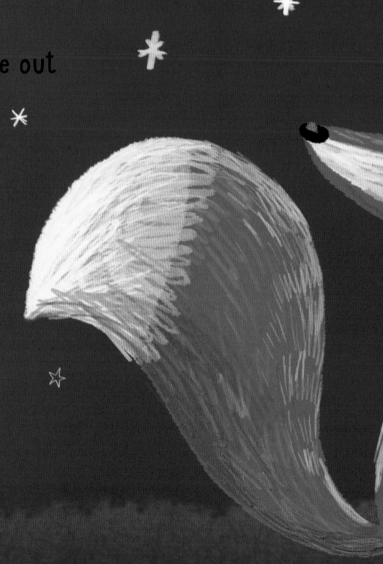

Rooster put his goggles on
and shouted, "Time to fly!"

He catapulted off the roof and up into the sky.

"I'll save you, hens!" he cried,
and Fox laughed,
"Really? What can you do?"

"Funny you should ask,"
said Rooster.

"CoCk-a-
dOoDle-
pOoooO!"

Everyone woke up at the sound
of Rooster CROWING!
So much poop was falling that
they thought it must be snowing!

The poor old fox was **flattened** by the massive

POoP attAcK.

He ran away and Rooster cried, "Get lost and don't come back!"

"You saved the day!" cheered Farmer Jill.
"But I don't understand—
How did you fly so high up there?
How *are* you going to land?"

But Rooster wasn't worried;
he didn't give a hoot.

The underpants he had
borrowed made . . .

...the perfect parachute!

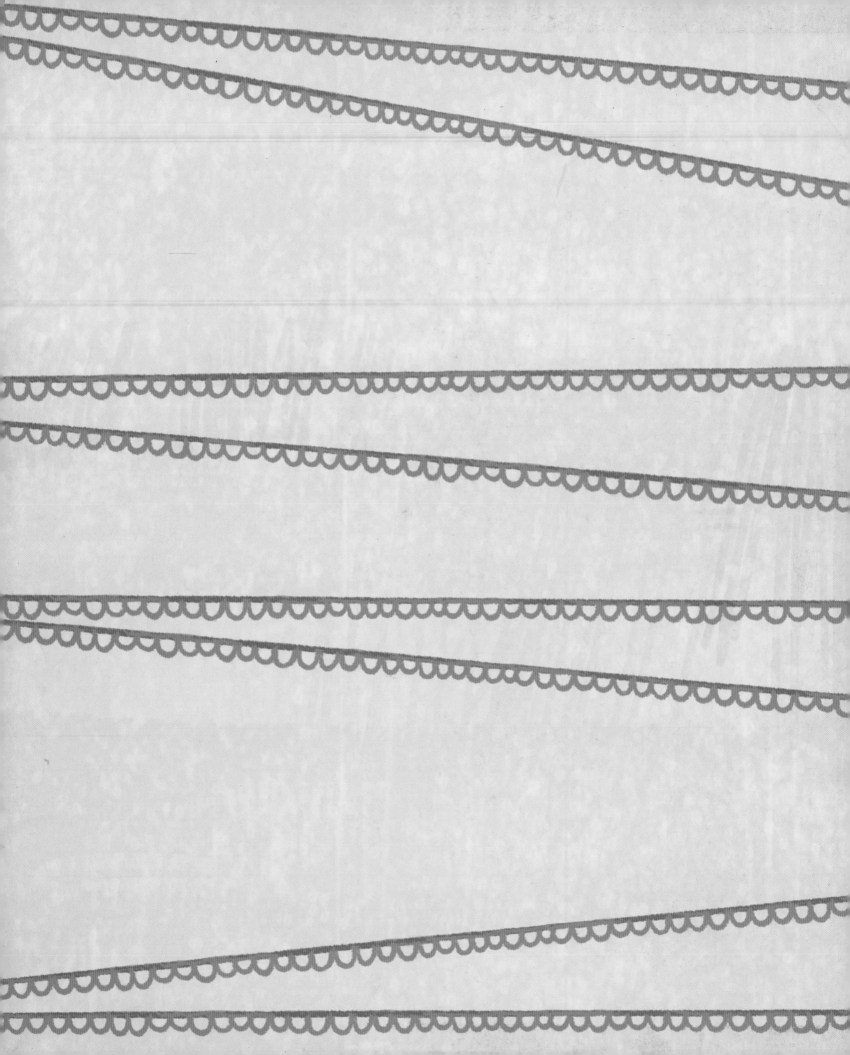